GHOSTBUSTERS ™

Adapted by John Sazaklis   ·   Illustrated by Alan Batson

Ghostbusters
Based on the Screenplay Written by Dan Aykroyd and Harold Ramis
Directed by Ivan Reitman

Ghostbusters: Who You Gonna Call?
Based on the Screenplay Written by Katie Dippold & Paul Feig
Based on the 1984 film "Ghostbusters" An Ivan Reitman Film
Written by Dan Aykroyd and Harold Ramis
Directed by Paul Feig

🍄 A GOLDEN BOOK · NEW YORK

Ghostbusters TM & © 2016 Columbia Pictures Industries, Inc. All Rights Reserved. Published in the United States by Golden Books,
an imprint of Random House Children's Books, a division of Penguin Random House LLC, 1745 Broadway, New York, NY 10019,
and in Canada by Penguin Random House Canada Limited, Toronto. The books that appear herein were also published separately by
Golden Books as *Ghostbusters* and *Ghostbusters: Who You Gonna Call?* in 2016. Golden Books, A Golden Book, A Big Golden Book,
the G colophon, and the distinctive gold spine are registered trademarks of Penguin Random House LLC.
randomhousekids.com
ISBN 978-1-5247-1487-1 (trade) — ISBN 978-1-5247-1488-8 (ebook)
Printed in the United States of America
10 9 8 7 6 5 4 3 2

When there's something strange haunting you, like ghosts and spooks and specters, and things that go bump in the night . . . **"Who you gonna call?"**

THE GHOSTBUSTERS!

It all began when three scientists named **Peter Venkman**, **Ray Stantz**, and **Egon Spengler** discovered that ghosts were real . . . *and* a real problem for New York City! They started a ghost-catching business called Ghostbusters.

When the alarm rings, they grab their proton packs and ghost traps. Then they race to the scene of the disturbance in their souped-up ghostbusting-mobile, **Ecto-1**.

The Ghostbusters realized that things were getting a little weird when they answered a call at a fancy uptown hotel. Ray spotted something he'd never seen before—a hungry green ghost named **SLIMER**.

He's an ugly little spud!

Ray chased Slimer right into Peter—

SPLAT!

HE SLIMED ME!

Using his **PKE** (psychokinetic energy) meter, Egon tracked Slimer to the hotel's ballroom. Egon warned the Ghostbusters not to cross their proton packs' streams. "It would be bad," he explained.

This ghost is toast!

The Ghostbusters quickly snared Slimer in a tangle of proton beams and sucked him into one of their traps!

Soon more and more ghosts appeared, scaring up trouble all over town.

Peter, Ray, and Egon needed help, so they hired a man named
Winston Zeddemore. Winston chased
ghosts across the city as a Ghostbuster!

But where were all the ghosts coming from . . . ?

The answer to that question could be found uptown. A supernatural cloud above a high-rise apartment building was drawing in ghosts from another dimension!

One day, a young musician named **Dana Barrett** was resting in her apartment. Suddenly, her favorite chair came to life and tried to grab her!

AIIEEEE!

And Dana's neighbor, accountant **Louis Tully**, almost became the chew toy of a snarling **Terror Dog**!

ROOAARR!

Something very strange was happening!

The Ghostbusters rushed to the rescue! At the top of the building, they found Dana and Louis—and a powerful being named **Gozer**!

"Whatever it is, it will have to get past us!" Peter declared.

Suddenly, Gozer transformed Dana and Louis into two growling Terror Dogs with glowing red eyes! Then the villain exclaimed,

"Choose the form of the Destructor!"

The Ghostbusters fired proton beams at Gozer, but it vanished into thin air. Suddenly, a spooky voice boomed, **"The choice is made!"**

"Whoa!" Peter shouted, looking at his teammates. "Did you choose anything?"

"I . . . I just couldn't help it," Ray stammered.

LOOK!

IT'S THE STAY PUFT MARSHMALLOW MAN!

Ray hadn't meant to, but he had thought of it. Now the Destructor had taken the form of a marshmallow man hundreds of feet tall!

"There's something you don't see every day," Peter joked as the giant marched toward them.

The Stay Puft Marshmallow Man climbed the building, reaching out with his delicious puffy hand to grab the Ghostbusters!

Egon came up with a radical idea: "We'll cross the streams."
The Ghostbusters combined the streams from their proton packs into one
massive blast . . . and aimed it right into the portal Gozer had opened.

Heat from the explosion roasted the Stay Puft Marshmallow Man.
Everything was covered in fluffy white goo. But it had worked—
the portal was closed.

Dana and Louis returned to normal, and the city was saved!

The heroes were greeted by thousands of cheering fans.
"I love this town!" Winston said.
Now the city knew exactly who to call—

THE GHOSTBUSTERS!

GHOSTBUSTERS!

GHOSTBUSTERS!

GHOSTBUSTERS!

GHOSTBUSTERS!

GHOSTBUSTERS™

WHO YOU GONNA CALL?

$$\log \frac{M_x}{M} = \frac{3(4\pi)^2}{22(1+3C^2)} \left[\frac{1}{e^2} \cdot (1+C^2)\frac{1}{g_3^2} \right]$$

$$\log \frac{M_x}{M} = \frac{6\pi}{11(1+3C^2)} =$$

Proton Decay? Gauge

(N) → N^2 | Bosons

P_x / RA(NO · RM)aIS + UDIes/

Erin Gilbert, Abby Yates, and Jillian Holtzmann were scientists in New York City who studied ghosts. They believed ghosts were real, but they didn't have any proof. They were determined to change that by making contact with the spirit world.

Erin had heard that the old Aldridge mansion was haunted, so she got the team together to investigate. Inside they found a *REAL GHOST*, and it *wasn't* scary at all! In fact, the ghostly lady was eerily beautiful. Erin approached it and said, "She looks so peaceful!"

But in a flash, the ghost turned nasty and sprayed slime all over her.

Abby was thrilled. "Ghosts *are* real!" she said. "That means they could be all over New York!"

With more and more ghosts beginning to haunt the city, Erin, Abby, and Holtzmann became **GHOSTBUSTERS**. Even though their office was above an old Chinese restaurant, and their receptionist, **Kevin**, wasn't very helpful, *and* they didn't have a car, the team was ready to start ghost hunting.

Holtzmann got busy. She went to work creating **proton packs** and **traps**. "If we're gonna catch ghosts," she said, "we're gonna need a lot of juice!"

The next day, Patty Tolan, a subway employee, followed a man named **Rowan** into a train tunnel. He was doing something suspicious with a strange device that started to spark and glow.

A frightening ghost named **SPARKY** appeared, scaring Patty out of her wits! But she knew who she could call for help.

After meeting the Ghostbusters, Patty joined the team. She had read books about New York and knew the city better than anyone. Patty borrowed uniforms for the team from her subway job, and she even got them a car. They named it **Ecto-1**.

Now they were officially ready for business.
First stop: a supernatural disturbance at a
heavy-metal concert.

The Ghostbusters arrived at the concert hall, where a menacing ghost named **MAYHEM** had trashed the stage. Erin shouted, "Let's crash this paranormal party!"

The team used their proton beams to hold Mayhem while
Holtzmann threw down her trap to catch the monstrous ghost.

The crowd went wild! They
thought it was part of the show.

Backstage at the concert, the Ghostbusters found another device like the one Patty had seen in the subway tunnel. Rowan was there, too! When he ran off, the Ghostbusters followed him to the Mercado Hotel, where he worked as a janitor.

"What are you up to?" Abby asked, tracking him down to his workshop in the hotel's basement.

"My machines have finally broken the barrier between the spirit world and ours!" he cackled as he unleashed a horde of horrible ghosts!

The ghosts from Rowan's portal poured into the streets. The Ghostbusters followed them and found themselves in the middle of an eerie Thanksgiving Day parade with giant balloon ghosts!

Rowan's machine turned him into a ghostly ghoul, too!
He ordered his marching mob to attack the Ghostbusters.
"That's a lot of creepy!" Patty exclaimed.

Holtzmann launched a proton grenade that blew the nearest nasties into puddles of ectoplasmic ghost goo.

The Ghostbusters fired up their proton packs and fought their way through the ghosts.

CRACKLE!

POP!

Rowan was furious. He transformed himself into a giant ghost and tried to stomp the Ghostbusters!

The team made a narrow escape.

"We need to close that portal!" Abby cried. The Ghostbusters combined their proton power into one concentrated stream of energy aimed at the portal.

Let's light it up!

KA-BOOM!!

There was a mighty explosion, and then the portal began to pull the spirits back into their own dimension.

Unable to escape its pull, Rowan vanished into the swirling portal, too!

The Ghostbusters had single-handedly saved the city from paranormal peril.
Now everyone in New York knew exactly who to call!